For Harriet and Toby—M. R.

For Mum and Dad—E. F.

First published in paperback in Great Britain by HarperCollins Children's Books in 2016
First published in hardback in 2016

1 3 5 7 9 10 8 6 4 2

ISBN: 978-0-00-816479-9

HarperCollins Children's Books is a division of HarperCollins Publishers Ltd.

Text copyright © Michelle Robinson 2016
Illustrations copyright © Emily Fox 2016

Visit our website at: www.harpercollins.co.uk

Printed in China

MIX
Paper from
responsible sources
FSC™ C007454

FSC™ is a non-profit international organisation established to promote
the responsible management of the world's forests. Products carrying the
FSC label are independently certified to assure consumers that they come
from forests that are managed to meet the social, economic and
ecological needs of present and future generations,
and other controlled sources.

Find out more about HarperCollins and the environment at
www.harpercollins.co.uk/green

Elephant's Pajamas

Michelle Robinson

Illustrated by Emily Fox

HarperCollins *Children's Books*

Elephant's inbox said "NEW MAIL."
He clicked on it, excited . . .

stairs . . .
the
up
right
charged
Elephant

and rummaged through his clothes.
An old shirt and some underpants.
"I can't show up in *those*!"

Elephant checked his Zoogle page . . .

Everyone was there.
And every single animal
knew just what
they would wear . . .

Donkey's jammies looked divine.

There were bunnies all over Bear's.

Everyone had pajamas—in fact . . .

they all had *spares!*

Flamingo's were pink . . .

Zebra's striped.

Dog's spare pair was **blue**.

Even Hippo had two onesies.

Oh, what would Elephant do?!

"Just go to the store!"
said Llama.

So Elephant left the house.

"I need new sleepwear
—jumbo size!
"Now let me see,"
said Mouse.

FITTING
ROOM

Elephant waited . . .

"How's this, Sir? It's big, but rather frilly."
He tried it on, but not for long.

It looked extremely silly.

Elephant thought outside the box. He shopped around a bit.

He searched.

He stretched.

He squashed.

He squeeeeeezed!

But nothing seemed to fit.

Elephant sat, and Elephant cried.
He clicked RSVP . . .

Well, maybe *elephants* go to sleep,
but Zoogle never does.

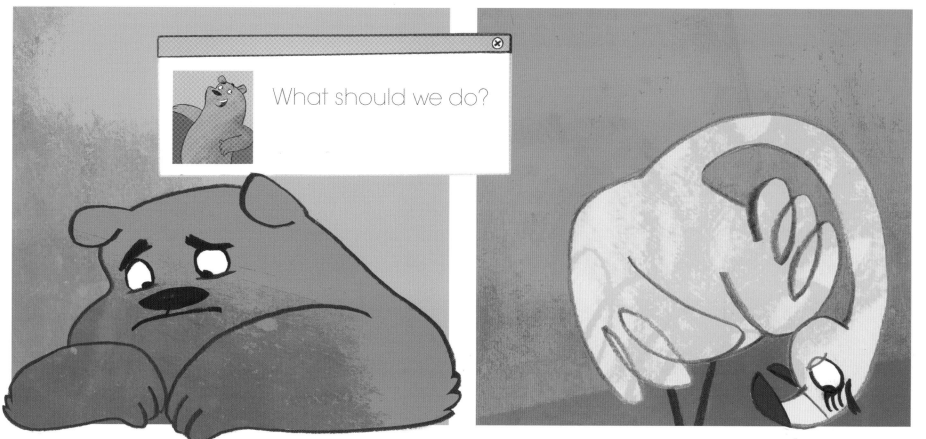

When Elephant's friends saw his message . . .
Oh! What a fuss there was!

"Right," said DonKey.
"Listen up—he says he isn't going.
I have a plan: come over to mine.
I hope you're good at SEWING."

Saturday night came by so fast.
Elephant sat at home.
No party, no cake, no games, no friends.
No pajamas, just . . .

Spare pajamas?
Not any more—just one pair, for a friend.

One happy Elephant, ready for bed.

Party on . . .

Sweet dreams!

The End.